HOW I BEAT MY BULLY

WRITTEN BY
NIELS VAN HOVE

ILLUSTRATED BY JULIANE ENGELHARDT

A STORY INSPIRED BY TRUE EVENTS

Published in Australia by Truebridges Media

First published in Australia 2019
Copyright © Niels van Hove 2019

National Library of Australia Cataloguing-in-Publication entry
Creator: Van Hove, Niels
Title: How I Beat My Bully
ISBN: 978-0-6480859-9-7 (eBook)
ISBN: 978-0-6480859-7-3 (Paperback)
ISBN: 978-0-6480859-8-0 (Hardback)

Target Audience: For primary school age
Subjects: Juvenile fiction. Confidence in children. Self-esteem. Bullying

Cover layout and illustrations by Juliane Engelhardt
Typesetting by Nelly Murariu (PixBeeDesign.com)
Printed by Kindle Direct Publishing

Disclaimer
All care has been taken in the preparation of the information herein,
but no responsibility can be accepted by the publisher or author for
any damages resulting from the misinterpretation of this work.
All contact details given in this book were current at the time of publication,
but are subject to change.

TO THE BRAVE LUCIA

1

HI, I'M ALICE.

THIS IS MY STORY ABOUT

HOW I OVERCAME

BEING BULLIED.

2

BEING BULLIED FEELS HORRIBLE.

IT WAS THE WORST THING THAT EVER HAPPENED TO ME.

BULLYING IS NASTY AND IT IS NEVER EVER OK!

3

BEING EXCLUDED ONCE, ACTING MEAN, OR A SINGLE FIGHT OR ARGUMENT IS NOT BULLYING.

BULLYING IS WHEN THIS HAPPENS OVER AND OVER AGAIN.
IT IS DONE TO HURT YOU AND CONTROL YOU.

YOU CANNOT ALWAYS SIMPLY KNOW WHO THE BULLY IS.

CAN YOU TELL **WHO THE BULLY IS** IN THIS GROUP?

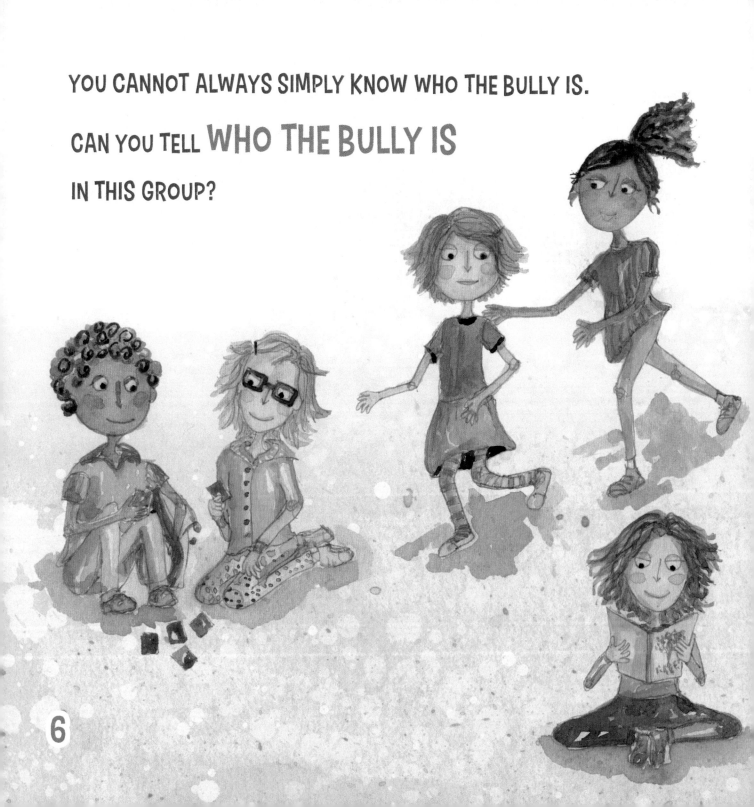

7

THE PERSON I THOUGHT WAS MY FRIEND, TURNED OUT TO BE A
BULLY. AT FIRST, WE WERE PLAYING WITH OUR OTHER FRIENDS.

THEN SHE STARTED TO CALL ME NAMES. 'YOU'RE DUMB. YOU'RE A LIAR. YOU'RE UGLY, AND YOU'RE NOT MY FRIEND.'

THE MEAN THINGS SHE SAID **HURT ME.** IT MADE ME FEEL SAD

AND UNSURE ABOUT MYSELF.

10

SHE WOULD **EXCLUDE** ME FROM PLAYING WITH MY FRIENDS' GROUP. I FELT **LEFT OUT** AND **ALONE.**

THIS WENT ON FOR WEEKS. THEN WEEKS

BECAME MONTHS. I DIDN'T

TELL ANYONE.

SOMETIMES I THOUGHT IT WAS MY FAULT.

IT WAS NOT, BUT THAT'S WHAT THE

BULLY TRIES TO MAKE YOU THINK.

AT HOME I STAYED IN MY ROOM.

I DIDN'T WANT TO GO TO SCHOOL.

I QUIT MY DANCE CLASSES.

I EVEN TOLD MY MUM I DIDN'T WANT TO LIVE ANYMORE.

ONE DAY THE BULLY

PUSHED ME

AGAINST THE WALL.

16

I FELL OVER AND HURT MYSELF
BADLY. THAT WAS IT!

I'D HAD ENOUGH!
I KNEW I HAD TO DO
SOMETHING ABOUT IT.

I TOLD MY MUM
EVERYTHING.

AT LEAST I DIDN'T HAVE
TO DEAL WITH IT
ALONE ANYMORE.

18

EVEN IF YOU DON'T
FEEL LIKE TALKING
ABOUT YOUR BULLY,
IT IS BETTER TO TELL
**SOMEONE YOU
TRUST** ABOUT
WHAT IS HAPPENING.

19

MY MUM AND I STARTED TO READ BOOKS
ABOUT HOW TO DEAL WITH BULLIES.

WE LEARNED THAT DEEP INSIDE,
THE BULLY IS OFTEN INSECURE AND
HAVE BEEN HURT THEMSELVES.

THIS IS SAD, BUT IT IS STILL
NEVER OK TO BULLY!

I LEARNED THAT I CAN MAKE MYSELF LOOK STRONG.
STAND TALL, MAKE EYE CONTACT, AND SPEAK CLEARLY.
SAY, 'STOP! I DON'T LIKE THAT.'

MY MUM HELPED TO MAKE SURE I WALKED TO SCHOOL WITH OTHER FRIENDS, SO I FELT SAFE.

I REALISED MY **BULLY ENJOYED** MY REACTION. THAT'S WHAT MADE HER FEEL IN **CONTROL** OF ME.

I DECIDED TO STOP GIVING MY BULLY ATTENTION. IF SHE APPROACHED ME, **I IGNORED** HER AND WALKED OFF.

MY BULLY REALISED I CARED LESS ABOUT HER. BULLYING SOMEONE WHO IGNORES YOU IS NOT MUCH FUN. SHE STARTED TO LEAVE ME ALONE.

THIS MADE ME FEEL STRONG. I REALISED THAT INSIDE, I ACTUALLY WAS STRONGER THAN MY BULLY.

I STARTED FEELING BETTER.

I JOINED DANCE CLASS AGAIN. MY MUM

ORGANISED PLAY DAYS WITH OTHER FRIENDS.

I KNEW I WAS SPECIAL, KIND, AND FUN TO PLAY WITH. I WAS HAPPIER AND GOT MY **CONFIDENCE** BACK.

IT WAS SO GOOD TO **FEEL LIKE MYSELF** AGAIN.

I EVEN SHARED MY STORY AT A
PARENTS' INFORMATION NIGHT
AT SCHOOL.

THAT WAS SO SCARY.

MY STORY HELPED PARENTS UNDERSTAND
HOW I BEAT MY BULLY.

NOW THEY CAN SUPPORT THEIR
CHILDREN IF IT HAPPENS TO THEM.

ONE DAY, MY STORY MIGHT HELP YOU TOO.

NOTES FOR PARENTS

This story is based on real life experiences from a young Australian girl. At the time of the story, she was a third-grade student. This is *her* story with some of *her* advice on how she beat *her* bully.

There are lots of aspects to bullying and there are many different types – verbal, physical, emotional, social, and cyberbullying. By no means do we suggest this story solves being bullied in every situation.

What her mum and the author want to provide, is a picture book that supports a conversation between adult and child about bullying. Telling a trusted person that you're being bullied is one of the most important steps to take for a child in this situation. It is also important for caretakers and educators to tune into any changes in behaviour and body language children might display.

Finally, we want to convey the message that although the main character had a terrible time, she discovered her self-worth and came out as a stronger, more resilient and confident young girl.

Peace

ABOUT THE AUTHOR

Niels is a father of two girls and lives with his wife in Melbourne, Australia. He is a mental toughness coach and author who enjoys getting the best out of individuals. With his books, he hopes to make a positive difference, promote conversation, and help children learn about confidence, resilience and a positive mindset.

ABOUT THE ILLUSTRATOR

Juliane is a Brazilian native from *Curitiba-Paraná,* a multi-artist and Olivia's mother. As a dance artist she teaches ballet classes and as a licensed visual artist, she works as an illustrator for publicity and cultural projects. She is co-creator of the Collective *"Nós em Traço",* where she works alongside three artist friends, seeking alternatives to art creation and education through the dialogue between body, movement and trace.

Kindness

Made in the USA
Las Vegas, NV
30 October 2023